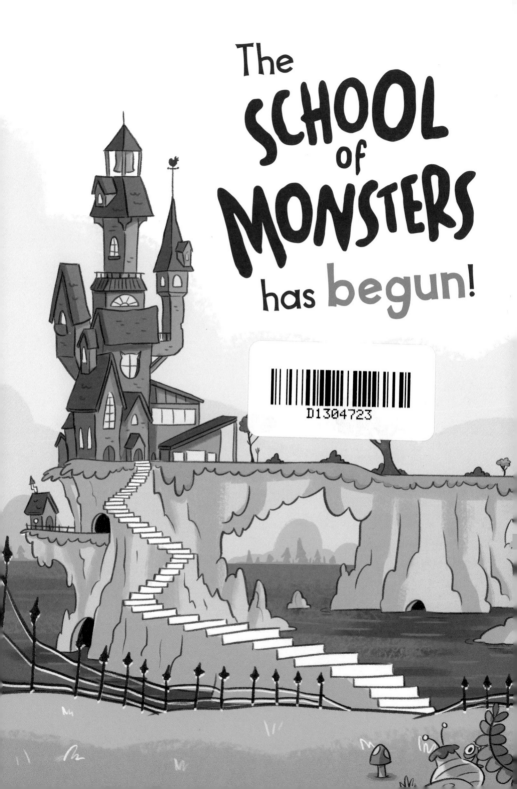

The
# SCHOOL
### OF
# MONSTERS
## has begun!

THIS BOOK
BELONGS TO

# SCHOOL OF MONSTERS

By
Sally Rippin

# JESS
## MAKES A
# MESS

Art by Chris Kennett

**Kane Miller**
A DIVISION OF EDC PUBLISHING

It's easy to tell where Jessica's **been**.

Jess leaves a trail that can often be **seen**.

SLOOOOP!

3

In winter she slides
like a smooth
block of ice,

but when it gets
hot it's not nearly
as **nice**.

Poor Jess becomes slimy and sticky like glue.

You can't get too close, or she might stick to **you!**

# Summer is hard, it's really quite tricky,

when all that Jess
touches gets gooey
and **sticky**.

She can't throw the ball as it sticks to her hand.

SPROING!

And when in the sandbox, she sticks to the **sand**!

By the end of the day,
just look at poor Jess.

She's stuck to her friends, and she's covered in **mess**.

# One hot summer day Jess waits at the gate

DON'T COME BACK

with Jamie, whose
mother is running
quite late.

# The friends see a mummy who gives them a **clue**

of how to stop Jessica
sticking like glue!

# They meet early morning the very next day

BA-DING
BA-DING

SNEAK

and hide from the others to go to sick **bay**.

SNEAK

They open the cupboards
to find what they **need,**

and wrap Jess up
tight with a superfast
speed.

WRAP

WRAP

Their teacher says, "Hi!" when Jamie sits down.

"Is this someone new?" he adds with a **frown.**

But Jamie just
giggles and pokes at
the **mummy**,

who holds in her
laughter and tucks
in her **tummy**.

"Where's Jess?" say the others. "She's part of our **game**!

We can't start without her. It won't be the **same!**"

Then Jess shouts,
"It's me!" and she giggles
with glee.

She unwraps some
bandages so they
can **see**.

"Oh Jess!" they all say.
"You look super **cool**!"

POFF

And guess what they
all wear the next day
at **school**?

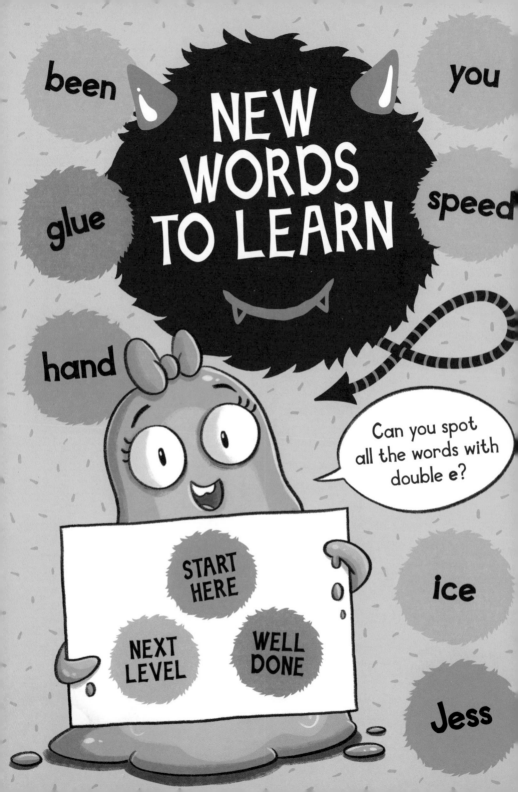

frown

mess

tummy

day

cool

late

same

tricky

school

bay

clue

mummy

seen

game

nice

see

down

need

glee

gate

sand

sticky

# HOW TO USE THIS BOOK

for adults reading
with children

## Welcome to the School of Monsters!

Here are some tips for helping your child
learn to read.

At first, your child will be happy just to
listen to you read aloud. Reading to your
child is a great way for them to associate
books with enjoyment and love, as well
as to become familiar with
language. Talk to them
about what is going on in
the pictures and ask them
questions about what they
see. As you read aloud, follow
the words with your finger from
left to right.

Once your child has started to receive some basic reading instruction, you might like to point out the words in **bold**. Some of these will already be familiar from school. You can assist your child to decode the ones they don't know by sounding out the letters.

As your child's confidence increases, you might like to pause at each word in bold and let your child try to sound it out for themselves. They can then practice the words again using the list at the back of the book.

After some time, your child may feel ready to tackle the whole story themselves. Maybe they can make up their own monster stories, too!

**Sally Rippin** is one of Australia's best-selling and most-beloved children's authors. She has written over 50 books for children and young adults, and her mantel holds numerous awards for her writing. Best known for her *Billie B. Brown*, *Hey Jack!* and *Polly and Buster* series, Sally loves to write stories with heart, as well as characters that resonate with children, parents, and teachers alike.

# HOW TO DRAW JESS

① Using a pencil, start with 2 circles for the eyes. Add eyebrows, eyelashes, and a small happy mouth.

② Draw a big upside-down **U** shape for her head, with a drip at each side.

③ Draw a straight line down at the front, and a bumpy line at the back.

④ Now connect the front to the back with a wavy line along the ground.

**5** Draw in 2 cone-shaped arms. One can be waving if you like!

**6** Time for the final details! Draw a bow on top of her head, and some drips for extra sliminess. Don't forget to put some on the floor!

**Chris Kennett** has been drawing ever since he could hold a pencil (or so his mom says). But professionally, Chris has been creating quirky characters for just over 20 years. He's best known for drawing weird and wonderful creatures from the *Star Wars* universe, but he also loves drawing cute and cuddly monsters – and he hopes you do too!

# WELCOME TO THE

## SCHOOL OF MONSTERS

**SCHOOL of MONSTERS**
By Sally Rippin
**MARY HAS THE BEST PET**
Art by Chris Kennett

You shouldn't bring a pet to **school**.
But Mary's pet is super **cool**!

# Have you read ALL the School of Monsters stories?

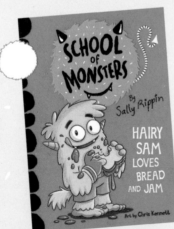

**SCHOOL of MONSTERS**
By Sally Rippin
**HAIRY SAM LOVES BREAD AND JAM**
Art by Chris Kennett

Sam makes a mess
when he eats **Jam**.
Can he fix it?
Yes, he **can**!

**SCHOOL of MONSTERS**
By Sally Rippin
**PETE'S BIG FEET**
Art by Chris Kennett

Today it's Sports Day
in the **sun**.
But do you think that
Pete can **run**?

Jamie Lee sure likes to **eat**! Today she has a special **treat** ...

When Bat-Boy Tim comes out to **play**, why do others run **away**?

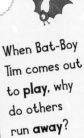

Some monsters are short, and others are **tall**, but Frank is quite clearly the tallest of **all**!

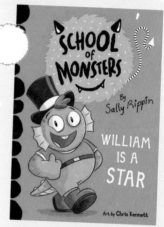

When Will gets nervous, he lets out a **stink**. But what will all his classmates **think**?

All that Jess touches gets gooey and **sticky**. How can she solve a problem so **tricky**?

No one likes to be left **out**. This makes Luna scream and **shout**!

Now that you've learned to read along with Sally Rippin's School of Monsters, meet her other friends!

Hey Jack!

Billie B. Brown

Down-to-earth, real-life stories for real-life kids!

# Billie B. Brown is brave, brilliant and bold, and she always has a creative way to save the day!

# Jack has a big heart and an even bigger imagination.
## He's Billie's best friend, and he'd love to be your friend, too!

# Jess Makes a Mess

First American Edition 2022
Kane Miller, A Division of EDC Publishing

Text copyright © 2022 Sally Rippin
Illustration copyright © 2022 Chris Kennett
Series design copyright © 2022 Hardie Grant Children's Publishing
First published in 2022 by Hardie Grant Children's Publishing
Ground Floor, Building 1, 658 Church Street Richmond,
Victoria 3121, Australia.

For information contact:
Kane Miller, A Division of EDC Publishing
5402 S 122nd E Ave, Tulsa, OK 74146
**www.kanemiller.com**
**www.myubam.com**

Library of Congress Control Number:
2021949061

ISBN: 978-1-68464-484-1

Printed in China through
Asia Pacific Offset

10 9 8 7 6 5 4 3 2 1

Hello, you!

Oh, please don't **look** inside the pages of this **book**.

# Turn around and
## quickly **run** ...